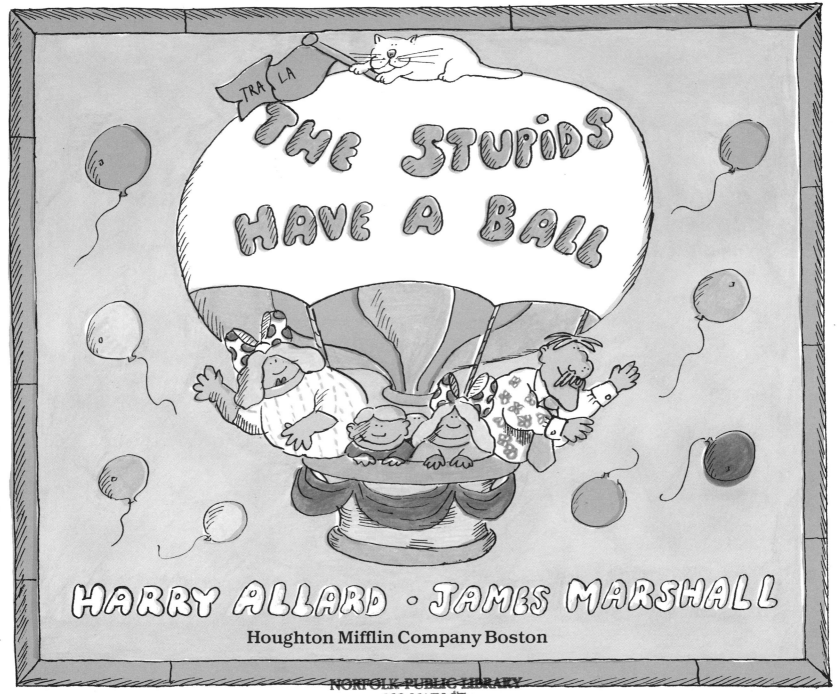

THE STUPIDS HAVE A BALL

TRA LA

HARRY ALLARD · JAMES MARSHALL

Houghton Mifflin Company Boston

Also by Harry Allard and James Marshall

The Stupids Step Out

Miss Nelson Is Missing!

Library of Congress Cataloging in Publication Data

Allard, Harry.   5-97   P donation AL $13.95
  The Stupids have a ball.

  SUMMARY: The Stupid family celebrates the children's awful report cards by inviting their relatives to a costume party.
  [1. Humorous stories.   2. Parties—Fiction]
I. Marshall, James, 1942-   joint author.
II. Title.
PZ7.A413Sq   [E]   77-27660
ISBN 0-395-26497-9

PRINTED IN THE UNITED STATES OF AMERICA.

Y 10

For Eve Fréjaville and Adolph Garza
with love

Report card time had rolled around again.
Mr. and Mrs. Stupid could hardly wait for
Buster and Petunia to get home from school.

"Hooray!" cried Mr. Stupid. "This time Buster and Petunia flunked *everything!*"

"And *that's* hard to do," said his wife.

The two Stupid kids beamed from ear to ear.

"This calls for a celebration!" declared Mr. Stupid.

"Why don't we have a costume ball and invite all our relatives?" said Mrs. Stupid.

"You know how they all like to get dressed up."

The Stupids' wonderful cat, Xylophone, was so excited her tail got stuck in her nose.

While Xylophone blew up party balloons,
Mr. and Mrs. Stupid and the Stupids' wonderful
dog, Kitty, wrote out the invitations.
"Oh dear," said Mrs. Stupid. "I don't know how
to spell Cousin Dottie Stupid's last name."
"That's a tough one all right," said her husband.

That afternoon, Kitty and Xylophone made punch in the kitchen.

"Their punch is always so tasty," whispered Mrs. Stupid. "I wonder what the secret ingredients are?"

The two Stupid kids smacked their lips.

"Time to put on our costumes!" Mrs. Stupid called out.

When Petunia saw her father's costume, she squealed with delight.

"I'm General George Washing Machine," said Mr. Stupid.

"I can see that, Daddy," said Petunia.

"Gosh!" cried Buster. "My Rudolf Rat
costume is missing!"
"Never mind," said his mother, who was wearing
some beautiful spaghetti. "You can always
make up your own outfit."

A loud quacking was heard in the yard.

"That must be Cousin Dottie Stupid,"
said Mrs. Stupid. "She's the only one
in the family who drives a duck."

Cousin Dottie was always the first to arrive
at parties.

"This duck really *moves*," said Cousin Dottie.

Soon other members of the Stupid family began arriving.

"My, my," said Mr. Stupid. "I've never
seen so many Stupids together in one room."
"There's Uncle Angus MacStupid,"
said Mrs. Stupid.
"Which one is he?" said her husband.

"Oh look!" squealed Petunia. "It's
Grandfather Stupid!"
Grandfather Stupid came down the chimney.
He was dressed as the Easter Bunny.
"Ho, ho, ho," he said.

The Stupids' guests were all enjoying
themselves immensely.
And everyone thought little Ichabod Stupid
was very cute when he dangled his toes
in the punch.

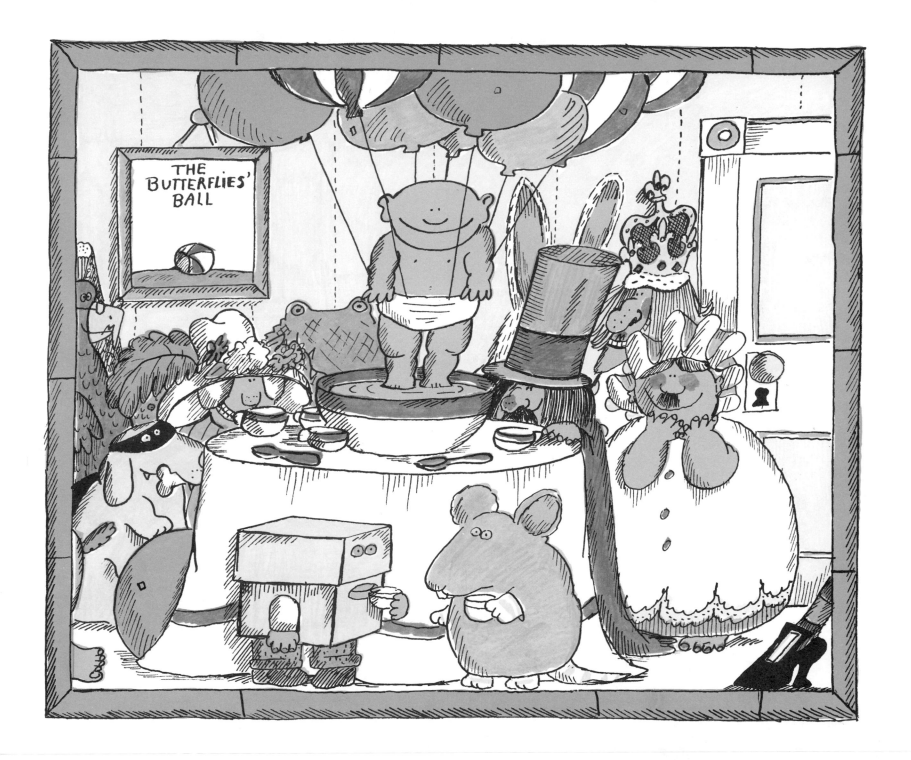

But Grandfather Stupid was having
the most fun of all.

"You sure can polka, Dot," he said.

When the ball was over and the last guest was leaving, Mr. Stupid turned to his wife. "Did you notice that we were the only ones wearing costumes?" he said. "The other Stupids came in their everyday clothes."

"Oh dear," said Mrs. Stupid. "I forgot to mention that it would be a *costume* ball."

"Never mind," said Buster. "We all had a wonderful time, General."

"We always do," said Mr. Stupid, closing the door.

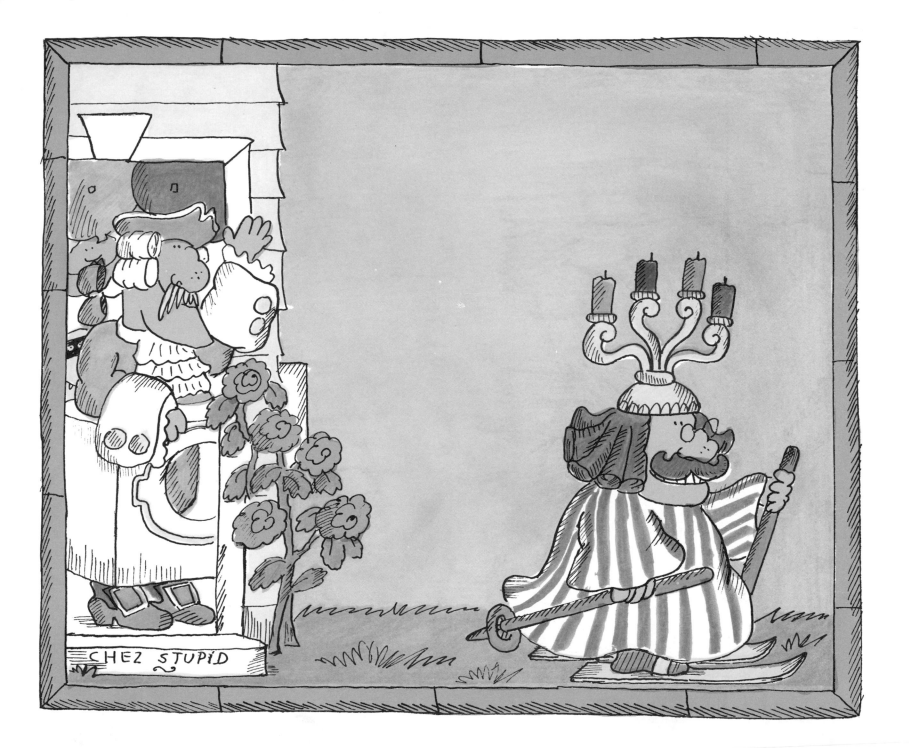